DRAGON CHILD

The Ruby Quest

GILL VICKERY

Illustrated by
MIKE LOVE

A & C BLACK
AN IMPRINT OF BLOOMSBURY
LONDON NEW DELHI NEW YORK SYDNEY

DRAGON CHILD

...o Patrick, the newest DragonChild

First published 2014 by A & C Black,
an imprint of Bloomsbury Publishing Plc
50 Bedford Square
London WC1B 3DP

www.bloomsbury.com

ISBN 978-1-4729-0433-1

A CIP catalogue for this book is available from the British Library.

Printed and Bound by CPI Group (UK) Ltd, Croydon CR0 4YY

1 3 5 7 9 10 8 6 4 2

FSC
www.fsc.org

MIX
Paper from
responsible sources
FSC® C020471

Northern Sea

Fellhof
‡

East Eldkeiler
Mts

Drakelow Mts
★

Eastern Sea

Kulafoss

Drangur ◻

Holmurholt

Askarlend ◻

Roornhof

Southern Sea

The Story So Far...

The High Witches stole the DragonQueen's jewels of power and drove the mighty beasts away. In revenge, a dragon kidnapped the youngest witch's child. Raised by dragons and tormented for being a 'witch-brat', Tia sets out to prove herself a true DragonChild by retrieving the jewels. She is helped by her DragonBrother, Finn, and the jackdaw Loki. Finn can blend invisibly into any background.

Tia has the emerald, which grants the power to talk to animals, the opal, which lets its owner change shape, the topaz, which controls the weather and the sapphire, which can transport the holder anywhere in the blink of an eye.

Finn safeguards the jewels, except for the emerald, which Tia keeps with her so that she can talk to Loki. By accident she made the sapphire take her to Askarlend, ruled by High Witch Hyldi. Hyldi has the ruby, which enables her to stop time.

Tia is alone. Hyldi knows a thief is coming for her jewel. Tia is in greater danger than ever before.

Chapter One

Stop Thief!

As the sun rose over the town of Askarlend everything changed. Light spilling from windows and doors faded and noisy music fell silent. Tia crept through quiet streets lit by faint morning light and an eerie red glow from the ring of volcanoes surrounding the town. *It's like being the only person alive*, she thought.

She hurried down sprawling lanes towards the castle that spread untidily over a low hill in the centre of the town. She had to get into the castle somehow and find where the High Witch Hyldi kept the magic ruby that gave her the power to stop time.

She turned a corner and found herself face to face with a group of people wearing brightly coloured caps and carrying brushes and buckets.

'Hey!' A woman pointed at her. 'Isn't that the thief girl, Nadya – the one Lady Hyldi's offering a reward for?'

'A reward!' The man next to her dropped his bucket with a clatter and started to push his way through the group towards Tia.

'I saw her first!' The woman tripped the man up with her broom. He fell against her, she bumped into another man and the whole group tumbled down like ninepins.

Tia ran. She couldn't believe she'd been recognised so easily. It was lucky that the people who'd spotted her had been too busy fighting among themselves to stop and catch her. Other people would be cleverer. She had to find a way to make herself less conspicuous before anyone else recognised her.

When she'd left the bumbling group safely behind, she slowed to a walk.

More people wearing the distinctive caps were clearing up the town. There was a lot to tidy away. The night revellers had trailed rubbish and mess everywhere and the sweepers had to work hard collecting all the litter before brushing the flagstones then swabbing them down.

Tia kept to the shadows and planned what to do next. Her DragonBrother, Finn, and her friend,

Loki the jackdaw, didn't know where she was. She'd accidentally used High Witch Skadi's magic sapphire and it had brought her to Askarlend town. It was lonely without Finn and Loki but until they found her she would have to make her own way. She set her mouth in a determined line and headed towards the castle.

In the squares and open spaces of the town people had begun setting up stalls and arranging goods. They chatted and called to one another, taking no notice of Tia as she strolled past, making sure she looked as casual as them.

The castle was a gigantic, sprawling, ugly building, with gaudy pots hung all over the walls. Under the pots, smears of dirty ash streaked with bright colour trailed down the stone. Tia was surprised to see that the colourful splashes glimmered faintly with magic. Servants, scampering up and down ladders, were filling the pots with vividly coloured fire-rock that also sparkled with magic. That must be what lit up the castle at night – magic flashing through the darkness.

Tia pulled up the collar of her jacket to cover as much of her face as possible and walked up to the castle's iron-studded gate, trying to seem confident. The open gate had a poster nailed to it.

To her horror she saw that the poster showed a picture of her face.

HAVE YOU SEEN THIS GIRL?

Her name is Nadya.
Bring her to the Lady Hyldi
and claim a reward of
six hundred marks.

Six hundred marks – that was even more than High Witch Skadi had offered in the town of Iserborg. No wonder people were keen to catch her.

She pulled her collar higher still and strode through the gate, her heart beating fast. Once inside, she kept to the shadows under the walls. Even so, a man walking by stared at her, paused and said, 'You – wait!'

Tia knew what he wanted. The six hundred mark reward for her capture. She hurtled through the bustling courtyard, scattering hens and setting a dog barking. She swerved to avoid his gnashing teeth and ran straight into a line of washing. The more she twisted and turned and tugged at the damp clothes, the more she got entangled.

'What are you doing, girl?' A tall, strong woman grabbed her in one hand and started to unwind the washing with the other. Tia wriggled furiously.

'Keep still, you're dragging the clothes in the dirt!' The woman shook Tia and the clothes line fell to the ground. She squirmed out of the woman's grasp, grabbed a green cap from the washing and pelted away, cramming the cap over her hair as she ran. At least that would make her look like a proper Askarlian worker.

She darted inside a large wooden stable built against the castle walls. It was cool and shady and smelled of hay. Rows of empty stalls ran down one side, with a big box-stall at one end. The top half of its door was barred and, staring through the bars as though she'd like to bite Tia very hard, was a furious-looking horse.

Despite its flattened ears and swishing tail, the horse was beautiful, with its golden hide and creamy mane and tail. Tia longed to stroke its velvety nose. She went closer. The horse snaked its head at her.

'Another human come to annoy me,' the horse said, swirling her tail angrily and showing the whites of her eyes.

'I wouldn't do that,' Tia said.

The horse stamped and backed up a little. 'You can talk to me! You're a witch! Has that High Witch Hyldi sent you?'

'No!' Tia said indignantly. 'I'm only a hedge witch, that's why I can understand you.'

That was a lie. She kept the magic emerald that enabled her to talk to animals and birds tucked under her shirt, on a chain round her neck.

She risked going a bit closer to the bars. 'I know about horses because the Traders taught me. My special friend was a grey called Fari. I learned to ride on him.'

The golden mare eyed Tia warily. 'You don't look like a Trader, even though you're wearing Trader clothes.'

'The Traders found me abandoned and brought me up. They called me…' Tia thought quickly. She didn't want to be known by her false name of Nadya; that was on the posters. '…Sura,' she decided. 'What's your name?'

'Yufa.' The mare tossed her head.

Tia rummaged through her pockets and found an apple she'd bought in Iserborg. She offered it to the horse. 'Would you like this?'

'I might,' the mare said.

Tia carefully opened the door and held out the apple. Yufa, still eyeing Tia suspiciously, reached forward and took the fruit with soft lips.

Tia patted the horse's neck. 'Why are you so angry?'

Yufa stamped again and shook her mane. 'My rider, Shandor, brought me to Askarlend to run in the races. When the High Witch saw me she wanted me for herself. Shandor refused. She took him away and brought me here.'

'Where's Shandor now?' Tia asked.

'I don't know,' Yufa said sadly. 'Will you find him for me?'

Helping Yufa would make Tia's task of stealing the ruby much harder and more dangerous. She was going to refuse but the little mare looked so lost without her rider that she couldn't. Tia knew all about feeling lost. Besides, the Traders had always been kind to her. She had to help bring Shandor and Yufa together again.

'All right, I'll try,' she said.

Yufa butted Tia gently with her nose. 'Thank you.'

An angry voice outside the stable doors made the mare's head jerk up again and her eyes widen in fright. 'It's her – Hyldi! Hide!' she warned Tia.

Tia quickly shut the stall door, scurried into a corner of the next stall, threw straw over herself and lay still.

The stable doors opened.

Chapter Two

Time Bubbles

Tia peered through a gap between the wooden slats and saw two people come in. One was a big, burly man with deep creases of worry crinkling up his forehead so that his eyebrows almost met above his nose. The other person was Hyldi, the High Witch of Askarlend and Tia's fifth aunt.

Tia stared in amazement. The fearsome witch was tiny!

Hyldi strutted towards Yufa's box-stall like a bantam hen, as though swaggering would make her appear taller and more important. Her clothes were in gaudy shades of pink, yellow and purple, all mixed up together, and her fair hair was topped by a huge bun. It reminded Tia of a gigantic honey cake and she had to squash her lips together to stop herself from laughing.

Then Tia stopped laughing. The ridiculous bun was pierced by a golden comb mounted with a huge, shining red jewel. The magic ruby!

The High Witch stamped her foot like a little child. 'Why has no-one been able to tame this animal?' she shouted at the big man.

'She's a spirited horse and misses her rider.'

'You should beat the creature into behaving!'

The man shook his head. 'Beating won't help. The Traders have a special, secret way with their horses. I'm not sure we can ever tame her.'

'Then I'll go back to the Trader and get this secret out of him,' the witch shrieked. She elbowed her way past the man, who followed her silently.

The stable door banged shut and Tia went back to Yufa, feeling ashamed that she was related to this terrible woman. Hyldi was just as cruel as the rest of the High Witches. She hated them all.

Yufa was trembling. 'What was the witch shouting about?' she asked Tia.

'She's going to Shandor, to talk about you.'

The horse kicked out, making the stall shake. 'Follow her! Make sure she doesn't hurt Shandor.'

But I'm only a girl! Tia thought. *She's a powerful witch.* Still, if she did follow Hyldi, she might discover something useful about the ruby. 'All right,' she agreed and hurried back into the courtyard. It was busier now. Tia pulled her cap down firmly, and followed the witch into the castle.

Askarlend was the strangest of the five castles Tia had seen. It was just as muddled inside as out. Hyldi stormed past a huge dining hall, ornate chambers and lush dressing rooms. As she went by, people bowed, turning their eyes away from the glowering witch. Tia followed at a careful distance.

Hyldi entered a long, downward-sloping tunnel lit by pots of the magic powder. She passed an armoury and rooms where soldiers were practising fighting skills. That tunnel led into another, tucked away behind a bulge of rock. It wound round and round, dipping deeper as it went. The ground suddenly lurched under Tia's feet – the volcanoes were grumbling deep under the earth.

A strange, pulsing red glow lit up the darkness ahead. Tia wondered if it came from molten lava but as she followed Hyldi round a final bend and entered a vast cavern, she saw that it was caused by something quite different. She gasped in astonishment.

Dozens of huge, luminous red bubbles floated around the cavern, bumping into the walls, drifting high into the roof and down again.

Inside each bubble was a person.

Tia crouched behind a tumble of rocks and watched as Hyldi slid the comb from her hair. She held it by the ruby and pointed its sharp glittering prongs at one of the bubbles. It drifted towards her.

Inside it knelt a Trader, his hands held out, palms up, his mouth and eyes wide open, as though he was pleading. *Shandor*, Tia thought and shuddered. The poor man was frozen in time inside the red bubble, neither properly awake nor properly asleep.

Hyldi stabbed the bubble with the comb. It dissolved into shimmering red dust and the man fell at Hyldi's feet.

'Get up!' she ordered.

He shook his head as though waking from a nightmare and staggered to his feet.

'Tell me your secret – the secret you Traders use to control your horses – so that my Horsemaster can tame that wild golden mare.'

Shandor smiled grimly. 'There is no secret, Lady. Yufa can only be ridden by people she trusts. It will never be you or your minions.'

'Never is a long time, Trader,' Hyldi snarled. She lifted the comb and made sweeping movements with her hand. Long stands of red light from the ruby began to form another bubble round the

Trader. He stood proudly and waited for it to close around him. When it was done the High Witch waved the bubble away and stabbed the comb back into her bun.

'Pah! I *will* learn your secret, Trader,' she hissed. 'You and your horse *will* obey me, as all who live in Askarlend do.' Hyldi swung round and stormed back up the tunnel.

Tia waited until she'd gone then ran back to the stables.

'Did you find him?' Yufa asked, her golden hide twitching with worry.

'Yes.' Tia leaned against the stall and told Yufa what she'd seen. 'I'm sorry,' she said when she'd finished.

Yufa stamped. 'The witch and her people will never ride me!'

That reminded Tia of her DragonBrother. She often teased him about letting her ride him and he always said, *I'm a free dragon, not a horse!* But Yufa was a free spirit too; she decided who could ride her.

The horse stamped again, harder. 'Set Shandor free,' she demanded.

'I will.' The words were out before Tia could help herself. *I've got to steal the ruby anyway,* she thought. *I may as well use it once I've taken it.*

Guiltily, she remembered that she'd promised Finn never to use any of the jewels, apart from the emerald. They were so powerful they almost hypnotised anyone who possessed them. She'd discovered for herself that it was too easy for the jewels to make you do things you didn't mean to. That was why the enchanter from over the seas had given them to the dragons. They were the only creatures strong enough and wise enough to use them without causing harm. But what if using the ruby was the only way to undo Hyldi's cruel spell? Surely Finn would understand that?

Tia put an arm round the horse's neck and her cheek on its creamy mane. *I hope I can rescue Shandor without the ruby,* she thought.

The stable door opened and a man strode over to the box-stall.

'What d'you think you're doing, girl? Get out of there, now!'

Chapter Three

The Horsemaster and the Headwoman

It was the man who'd come to the stables with Hyldi. His face was pale and frightened. 'Move slowly, that horse is dangerous.'

He took a step closer to the stall and Yufa bared her teeth.

'There's nothing to worry about. She won't hurt me.' Tia patted Yufa and whispered, 'Remember, I promise I'll help Shandor.'

The little mare dipped her head and pushed gently at Tia. 'All right.'

'I'll be back with some apples later,' Tia said in a normal speaking voice.

She gave Yufa a last pat and left the box-stall. The man whistled softly.

'I don't know how you did that. It was almost as if you understood each other.'

Tia shrugged. 'The Traders taught me about horses.'

She was ready to run if she got the chance but the man was blocking her way. He stroked his stubbly chin. 'Hmm, you don't look like a Trader child, though you dress and speak like one. What's your name? Where are you from?'

'I'm Sura.' Tia recited her story about being a foundling baby rescued by the Traders; how she was parted from them in a fog and was going from town to town, seeking them. It seemed to satisfy him.

'I need a new stable-hand. She...' he nodded towards Yufa, 'kicked one and broke his leg. Would you like the job?'

'Yes,' Tia said tentatively, not sure she trusted this man. He seemed kind and honest but she'd met a man like that a few days ago and he'd betrayed her.

'Good. I'm Gunnar, the Horsemaster of Askarlend. No-one argues with me.'

Apart from Hyldi, Tia thought.

'You're under my protection while you're here.' A friendly grin split his weathered brown face. 'You might want to keep that cap pulled on tighter.'

So he *had* recognised her as the girl on the poster.

The cap had slipped. She yanked it back into place. 'Master Gunnar...'

The burly man held up his hand. 'I'm not interested in the six hundred marks.' His grin widened. 'Besides, Yufa here is the fastest horse in all Tulay. If you can ride her, I'll win far more than the reward the Lady Hyldi's offering.'

'I will,' Tia said confidently. 'But first, I promised Yufa apples. And I'm hungry too,' she added.

Gunnar let out a bellow of laughter that startled the horse. 'Come with me, Sura. My wife will give you apples – and breakfast.'

Still chuckling, the big man led Tia back into the castle. They passed the grand rooms, went down the rocky tunnels and climbed up again to the ground floor in another part of the castle.

Gunnar pushed at a thick wooden door that opened on a long, airy room with shuttered windows latched back to let in light. Tia wrinkled her nose at the sulphurous smell wafting in from the ring of volcanoes that surrounded Askarlend.

Tables stood in a neat line down the centre of the room, some with papers, plans and charts on them and others with scales and measuring cups. They didn't look magical, they looked practical.

'Where are we?' Tia asked.

'In the Headwoman's rooms. This is where she organises all that goes on in the castle.'

'She must be very important,' Tia said, wondering why Gunnar had brought her here.

'She is!' He grinned.

A tall woman bustled in, a bunch of keys jingling at her waist. It was the woman from the courtyard who'd untangled Tia from the washing. Tia slipped behind the Horse Master.

The woman didn't even glance at her; she was too busy glaring at Gunnar. 'What are you doing here, husband?'

He gave a deep rumbling laugh. 'I've brought my new stable hand to show you. Vanna, meet Sura.' He pushed Tia forward. For a moment she feared she'd been tricked again, and that the woman would snatch her and haul her off to Hyldi. But Vanna smiled warmly.

'She's hungry,' Gunnar told his wife.

'Children are always hungry – what has this one done to earn her breakfast?'

'Tamed Yufa.' The Horse Master winked at Tia.

'In that case,' Vanna's smile grew even broader, 'you deserve two breakfasts!'

'Could I have one breakfast and some apples for Yufa?'

Vanna twitched her snowy white apron straight. 'Frida!' she called and a small, cheeky-looking girl rushed in.

The Headwoman told her to bring to bring food. In no time at all Frida was back with a very large tray loaded with fresh bread, butter, cheese and fruit. Tia's mouth watered. Frida cleared a space at one of the tables and they all sat down while Tia had breakfast.

She hadn't eaten or slept since the previous evening, before she was accidentally transported to Askarlend by the magic sapphire, and she was famished and exhausted. She ate ravenously while Gunnar and Vanna talked about castle affairs. Frida chipped in from time to time, making them laugh with her sharp comments.

Tia's head nodded, drooped and finally rested on the table. She fell fast asleep over her breakfast.

Chapter Four

Kettil

'Wake up, Nadya!' a voice said.

Tia didn't want to wake up. The bed she was lying on was soft and warm.

'Nadya, time to get up,' the voice insisted.

'All right, I'm getting up!' Tia mumbled. She opened an eye and saw Frida.

'I knew you were that Nadya,' Frida said.

Tia yawned. 'No I'm not. Where am I? What're you doing here?'

'You're in the room next to mine. We're near Vanna and Gunnar's room. That way they can keep an eye on us.'

'Why?'

Frida tossed her red hair over her shoulder and grinned a crooked grin. 'I'm apprentice Headwoman so I need to be close to Vanna. And you're Nadya the thief so you need to be protected by Vanna and Gunnar.'

'I'm not Nadya.'

'Yes you are. I recognised you easily without the cap. And you answered me when I called you Nadya just now.'

Tia opened her mouth to protest but Frida held up her hand so sharply that she couldn't help shutting it again.

'I won't give you away. If Vanna wants to protect you, there's a reason.'

Tia had seen at breakfast that Frida worshipped Vanna and wouldn't ever disobey her. She decided she could trust this loyal girl too.

Frida handed Tia her cap. 'We're going out, Nadya. You'll need this.'

Tia took the cap. 'Call me Sura,' she insisted. 'Where are we going?'

Frida jumped off the bed. 'You've slept far into the day. It's too late now to start work so Vanna wants me to show you round the town. She's given you some marks to spend. Come out when you've changed.'

Then she was gone. Frida moved like a darting squirrel, faster than anyone Tia had ever known.

Tia felt anxiously in her jacket pocket. The sapphire bracelet was still there. She glanced at it quickly before looking away. She knew that if she looked into the jewel's blue heart she'd be horribly tempted to use it. She had to hide it.

The room was small, just a living and sleeping chamber with a little washing annex. It was furnished with a bed, a chair and a table – with her backpack and a bag of apples on it – a cupboard, and a small couch with cushions. Tia grabbed a cushion, bit open one end of a seam and pushed the bracelet inside. She put the cushion back on the couch.

She changed into the fresh clothes piled on the end of her bed and put her jacket back on. She was just pushing her feet into her boots when Frida poked her head round the door. 'Come on, plodder!'

Tia picked up the bag of apples and followed Frida into the town.

Askarlend was a noisy, brash trading centre, near to the port of Roornhof on the coast of the Southern Sea. The town was full of merchants and visitors from over the seas, all dressed in brightly coloured clothes. Stalls selling every kind of goods were packed along the streets and in the squares. Tia and

Frida wrinkled their noses as they hurried past fish stalls. Further on they stopped to buy honey cakes.

As well as food, stallholders sold silk and leather, metalwork and costly gems. One stall sold sunstones from Kulafoss and another precious saffron from Stoplar. Smaller stalls sold cheaper goods such as trinkets and games while even smaller booths, painted with moons and stars, promised to tell fortunes if you came inside.

'Don't bother with them,' Frida said scornfully. 'Let's go and see the fire-eaters.'

'Fire-eaters!' Tia liked the sound of that.

'And jugglers and acrobats,' Frida said. 'They're in West Gate Square.'

When they got there Tia recognised the square as the one she'd arrived in last night. Today it was packed with excited people gasping as acrobats performed impossible feats and fire-eaters breathed out streams of flame.

Tia was most impressed by the acrobats. She could make fire just by snapping her fingers, but she couldn't balance on one hand at the top of a pyramid of people.

She and Frida wandered through the noisy crowds until they found themselves near a gigantic statue of a troll.

'This statue is very mysterious,' Frida said. 'It appeared from nowhere last night.'

Tia tried not to laugh. She knew all about the troll because she'd brought it with her by accident from Iserborg. Once it reached Askarlend, the magic that made it live had drained away and it had turned back into an ordinary statue once again.

'It is mysterious,' Tia agreed, looking up at the troll's snarling face. A black bird landed on the troll's head. Tia squinted. It was Loki.

Tia snatched off her cap and waved it, jumping up and down in excitement at seeing her friend at last.

The jackdaw hopped down onto the troll's arm. 'There you are,' Loki squawked.

'Put your cap on,' Frida hissed. 'You'll be recognised if you're not careful!'

Tia tugged it back on.

'Bet I can get that bird,' a voice said behind her.

Tia turned. A hulking boy at the front of a group of children was swinging a sling, his eye on Loki.

'Go away, jackdaw,' Tia yelled. 'You're in danger!'

He flew off, zigzagging through the air so that boy couldn't get a good aim. His stone went wide. Some of the children jeered but most looked away or said, 'Bad luck.' He pushed them aside and marched angrily towards Tia and Frida.

The boy thrust his face in front of Tia's. 'What
d'you warn that bird for?'

Tia laughed and stood straight even though the
boy was taller and heavier than her. 'You think I can
talk to birds?'

The boy flushed. Some of his gang tittered. 'You
know what I mean – your shouting scared it off.'

Tia shrugged. 'You probably wouldn't have hit it
anyway. You were aiming all wrong.'

'What do you know?' he sneered.

Tia pulled her sling out of her pocket. 'I bet I can beat you any time.'

The group of children gasped and Frida stepped up beside Tia. 'Leave her alone, Kettil,' she said to the boy.

Kettil's face twisted in a sneer. 'Why should I?' he said to Frida. 'Just because you're apprentice Headwoman?'

'Because if you don't I'll report you to Gunnar.'

Kettil's face burned red with anger. His fists bunched and his eyes bulged. Frida and Tia stood their ground. Kettil grunted and swung away, his gang huddled protectively round him.

'I'm not sure I should've spoken that way,' Frida said. 'He might want revenge for making him look silly.'

It was just like being back in Drakelow with the dragonets tormenting her for being a witchbrat. Kettil even reminded her of Torkil, the worst of the dragonet bullies. Tia sighed, then grinned. She'd always got the better of Torkil – she could do the same with Kettil.

Chapter Five

The Race

'Let's forget about Kettil and take Yufa the apples,' Tia said.

Frida agreed and the two of them made their way to the stables. By this time the other horses were stabled too but the hands had finished for the night and no-one else was about.

Frida looked warily at Yufa. 'Won't she won't bite you?'

Tia shook her head and stepped up to the bars.

'Hello, Yufa. I've brought you those apples I promised,' she said.

Yufa gave a whicker of pleasure.

Frida drew in a sharp breath of surprise and Yufa flattened her ears.

'It's all right,' Tia reassured the horse. 'That's my friend Frida.'

'I don't want her to come in,' Yufa insisted, rolling her eyes.

'She's a bit nervous,' Tia fibbed to Frida. 'Why don't you wait over there?'

Frida stepped back several paces. Tia unlatched the box-stall door, confident that Frida was too far away to hear what she was going to say to Yufa.

'Don't go in, it's too dangerous!' Frida called, clutching her hands together as if she were wringing out washing.

Tia ignored her and went inside. She took an apple out of the bag and offered it to Yufa. The horse's soft lips nuzzled at her palm as they picked up the fruit.

'I'm going to be looking after you from now on,' Tia said. You'll let me ride you, won't you?'

The little golden mare agreed she would and finished off the apples.

Tia slapped her gently on the rump and left the box-stall. 'I'll see you tomorrow,' she said through the bars and Yufa breathed a smell of apples and sweet hay over her.

'How did you get her to behave?' Frida said, as they left the stables. Her eyes were wide with awe.

'It's the Trader way.' And Tia refused to say any more.

When they reached the castle Frida said, 'I'll show you around. It's easy to get lost in all the corridors and tunnels.'

Though Frida led Tia through the castle at dizzying speed she took care to explain the different levels. The ground floor was for daily living with places to eat, entertain, do business and sleep. Below that was a floor devoted to kitchens and food storage and under that, places for training soldiers. Under that again were more storage rooms.

Frida didn't mention the cavern of the red time bubbles.

Gunnar kept Tia busy for the next few days. She followed the daily routine: mucking out Yufa, exercising, feeding and grooming her. She rose early, did her jobs and ate breakfast with the other stable hands. She got on well with all of them, except for Kettil and his friends. They only glared at her without speaking as she went about her work.

She spent the evenings in the town with Frida and went to bed tired out. Tia badly wanted to give the sapphire to the jackdaw so that he could take it to Finn for safekeeping. And even more, she longed for news of the little dragon. But although she spotted Loki several times they never had a chance to speak.

Gunnar observed her closely as she worked with Yufa. Tia was sure he had some plan in mind, and she was right.

One morning, when the horses had been walked back from their exercise, the Horsemaster said to Tia, 'We'll try racing Yufa tomorrow.'

'A race!' Tia's eyes sparkled. She'd raced against Trader children at Drakelow where she lived with the dragons, but never on a horse as swift as Yufa. She couldn't wait.

And neither could anyone else. The whole castle was buzzing with gossip about Yufa taking part in the coming race. Tia wasn't the only one who hardly slept for excitement that night.

The next day was sunny and crisp with a clear sky. Even the volcanoes were only smoking gently without rumbling and shaking the ground.

When it was time for Tia to walk Yufa to the cinder track outside the castle, the little mare danced in excitement.

'Don't be too eager,' Tia said. 'Remember what we planned – let another horse take the lead, stay close and then pass.'

Yufa tossed her head making her creamy mane wave. 'I just want to run and run!' she said.

Tia patted the horse's neck. 'I just want to win!'

'You won't.' A boy on a chestnut horse sneered as he peeled off from the other riders and rode closer to Tia. It was Kettil. 'At least, not if you know what's good for you.'

Tia ignored him. She was going to enjoy this ride. They reached the starting line Gunnar had laid down with a thick stripe of white ash and lined up as best they could. A noisy crowd gathered round, watching the riders jostle their horses into position. Kettil forced his chestnut horse, Folski, next to Yufa. 'I warned you, don't try and win,' he threatened.

At that moment Gunnar started the race. The crowd cheered and the horses shot away. Yufa flew ahead of the field. This wasn't the plan! But at least they'd left Kettil behind. Tia grinned. He wouldn't like that. She crouched over Yufa's neck and concentrated on the race.

They flew round the first of the two laps and started on the second. Yufa was still out in front, only two horses closing the gap between her and the rest of the field: Kettil's Folski and a white horse called Drifa.

39

The sound of drumming hoofs grew nearer, voices yelled. Tia risked looking round. Folski was gaining fast, Drifa not far behind.

Tia gripped her knees tighter, bent lower over Yufa's neck. 'C'mon, half a lap – we can do it!' she shouted against the wind streaming in their faces. Yufa was too intent on hurtling to the winning post to answer.

'Ow!' Something stung Tia's leg and she almost lost her grip. The sting came again, more fiercely this time.

Kettil! He'd drawn level and was hitting her with his whip. The next blow came harder still and Tia struggled to keep on Yufa's back.

Kettil hit her again. She felt herself slipping.

Suddenly Loki was flapping and darting round Kettil's head. Folski shied in alarm, and bucked Kettil off. The bird soared away.

'Now's our chance!' Tia yelled to Yufa, who took the bit in her mouth and ran like a winter wind. They thundered over the line far ahead of Drifa and the rest of the field.

'Yes!' Tia yelled as they slowed down. 'We won!'

'I told you we would,' Yufa panted. 'Are you all right?'

'I think so.' Tia slid from the horse's back and took a few steps. She was fine apart from her painful leg. 'It's just bruises.'

She led Yufa back to the line and the cheering crowd. Gunnar was waiting at the front, the High Witch beside him.

When Yufa saw Hyldi she stopped and refused to budge another inch. Hyldi's face tightened with anger.

'You girl, come here,' she ordered.

'Yes, Lady,' Tia said politely. She turned to Yufa and whispered, 'Let the man hold you while I talk to the witch.'

Yufa wasn't happy about it but she stayed still when Tia passed the reins to Gunnar.

'How is it that you can ride this horse?' Hyldi demanded.

'I was raised by Traders, Lady, and know their way with horses. They trust me, as they trust all Traders,' she added remembering what Shandor had said to the witch.

Hyldi must have remembered too. 'So they all say,' she muttered. She gripped Tia's shoulder hard. 'Child, you will train this horse to obey me.'

Tia wanted to shout, 'Never!' but reporting to Hyldi now and then might help her work out how to steal the ruby and free Shandor. 'I'll try my hardest, Lady,' she said meekly. 'It may take some time.'

'Time? Time is nothing to me.' The High Witch sneered and swept away, flanked by two guards. They made her look even smaller and sillier as she swaggered back to the castle.

Gunnar stroked his bristly chin thoughtfully. 'Take Yufa back to the stable and make her comfortable, then take yourself back to your room,' he told Tia. 'I'll tell Vanna to draw you a hot bath to ease those bruises Kettil gave you. We all saw what happened. It's no way for a rider to behave.

I'll deal with him. And you can have the rest of the day to yourself.'

He handed the reins back to Tia. 'It was strange about that bird though. It looked as if it deliberately flew at Kettil to stop him hitting you. Never seen anything like it.'

Shaking his head, Gunnar went to see the other riders and their horses.

Tia led Yufa back to the stables, washed her down, groomed her thoroughly and gave her food and water. When she'd straightened the little mare's bed she said, 'We showed you really can race.'

'I know,' Yufa said smugly through a mouthful of hay.

Smiling, Tia closed the box-stall door and limped wearily off for a warm bath to soothe her aches and pains.

Chapter Six

Bronze Horse, Jade Dragon

Frida was needed at the castle so Tia was free at last to search for Loki and give him a message for Finn. She tore a leaf from the book she carried in her backpack and wrote a note explaining what had happened to her and how much she missed her DragonBrother. Then she retrieved the sapphire bracelet from the cushion, wrapped it in the paper and tied up the whole thing with threads from the cushion's cover. She left one side poking out of the parcel like a handle. She hoped it wouldn't be too heavy for Loki to carry.

She set off for West Gate Square but stopped on the way at a Trader stall selling goods from far Cathay. There was a bronze horse that looked as if it were galloping through the sky, one back hoof supported by a flying bird.

'It's one of our finest pieces,' the Trader told her. 'Perhaps the Lady Hyldi will buy it. We all know how much she loves horses.'

DragonTeacher had told Tia and the dragonets that Hyldi was famous for two things: stealing the ruby of power, and her fearsome temper. He hadn't known about her passion for horses. It would explain why the High Witch had been so angry when Shandor refused to part with Yufa.

A jade medallion carved with a dragon chasing a creamy pearl caught Tia's eye. The pearl was the last magical jewel that Tia would have to recover for the dragons. The High Witch Ondine, Tia's own mother, had it. Tia touched the green stone gently with a fingertip.

The Trader's brown eyes crinkled in a friendly smile. 'I can see this has a special meaning for you. Would you like to buy it? The people of Cathay say that the dragon brings good fortune and the pearl guides you to the truth you are seeking.'

Tia shook her head. She didn't want anything to remind her that her mother was a High Witch. She said goodbye to the Trader and went to the stone troll, hoping that Loki would be there. He was, perched patiently on its shoulder. Tia waved and pointed the way to a smaller, quieter square. They met there by a fountain.

'I suppose you want me to run errands to that DragonBrother of yours,' Loki said. 'Have you got the sapphire?'

Tia showed him the package. Loki eyed it. 'Are you sure you don't want an eagle to take it?'

'You can manage, I know you can.' Tia stroked his ruffled feathers. 'I miss you and Finn.'

'He misses you. He spends most of his time practising his camouflage to take his mind off it. He's getting very good. I think he could fool the spell boundaries completely now.'

'He'd better not try!' Tia said. 'That spell the High Witches cast to protect their lands is very powerful. I know he's fooled it before for a short while but he didn't have to keep it up for very long.'

She shuddered. The spell was very strong. It had overcome the great dragon Andgrim. Tia didn't want to think of the same thing happening to her DragonBrother, who was far smaller than Andgrim.

She turned her attention to Loki.

'Thank you for stopping that boy from hitting me. Yufa and I wouldn't have won the race without your help. It was very brave of you.'

'Yes, it was.' Loki grasped the loop of bracelet with both claws. 'Try not to get into trouble again. I might not be able to rescue you next time.'

He took off clumsily, flew around to get his balance and then was off, away over the town. Tia watched till he was just a tiny black speck in the sky. She wished she could fly away to Finn too. But she had the ruby comb to steal and Shandor to set free. There was no time to feel sorry for herself. She returned to the bustling centre of the town and went to look for honey cakes to share with Frida.

After she'd bought the cakes Tia walked past the Trader's stall on her way back to the castle. A small gathering was clustered around it with Hyldi and her two guards at the front. The witch, her eyes narrowed greedily, had her hands on the bronze horse.

'I want this horse,' she said to the Trader. 'You will deliver it to my palace immediately.'

'Of course.' The Trader bowed a very small bow. 'And will the honoured lady pay me now, or later, at the palace?'

'Pay!' Hyldi's eyes bulged in fury. 'You will present it to me as a gift, and be grateful!'

'I am a Trader, Lady Hyldi. The horse is for sale.'

People gasped. 'The Lady Hyldi will be so angry with him for saying that,' a man murmured.

Tia thought he was right but Hyldi was very rich – why shouldn't she pay for the horse?

The witch's hand flew to the ruby comb in her hair. It blazed red and the world came to an abrupt halt. Birds were suspended in the air; people stood with their mouths open, halfway through saying something, or paused in mid-stride. Hyldi had stopped time throughout the town.

Why aren't I frozen too? Tia wondered. It could only be because she was a witch, like Hyldi.

Hyldi reached into the Trader's stall and took a necklace, several rings, a circlet made of golden leaves and the jade dragon. She put them all in a bag.

She's a thief! Tia thought. *How dare she steal from an honest Trader?*

Of course, Tia was a thief too but she was only stealing the jewels from the High Witches so that she could return them to their real owner, the DragonQueen. She wasn't taking things just because she wanted them for herself.

Hyldi stepped back, a sneer twisting her face, and stroked the ruby. Another red flash brought

the world back to life. Time began again from the exact moment it had stopped. Only Tia was aware of what the witch had done.

'Take this horse to the castle,' Hyldi ordered one of her guards.

He picked up the bronze horse and the Trader stood by helplessly as Hyldi and her guards walked away. The small crowd around the stall melted away, leaving just a single man. He wore a long cloak and a wide-brimmed hat that shaded half his face. Fair hair straggled greasily over his shoulders.

'Well, Trader,' the man said, 'seeing that the Lady Hyldi has taken your valuable bronze horse, perhaps you'll sell me one of your real ones now?'

'Never,' the Trader said. 'We'd never sell a horse to one of your kind.'

The man's face flushed. 'Then perhaps I should follow the example of the Lady Hyldi and *take* what I want.' He pulled his cloak around himself and slouched away.

What had the Trader meant by 'your kind'? Puzzled, Tia watched the cloaked man. She saw two soldiers approach him. The men were too far away for Tia to see clearly but she thought the soldiers were Hyldi's guards. They talked and then the man in the cloak followed the soldiers in the direction of the castle.

Tia was sure they were up to no good. She followed them.

Chapter Seven

Bandits!

The soldiers and the cloaked man strode along the castle tunnels, down to the deepest level. Tia thought they were going to the cavern of time bubbles but they stopped before they reached it, and a soldier hammered on an iron-banded door.

'He's here, Lady,' he boomed.

'Well send him in, fool!' Hyldi's voice shrieked.

The guards let the cloaked man in, closed the door and stood to attention.

'It's about time those arrogant Traders got what's coming to them,' one of the guards said.

The other gave a harsh snort of laughter. 'And Bragi is the one to do it!'

'This time tomorrow they'll be sorry.'

Tia chewed her lip. The cloaked man, Bragi, and Hyldi were hatching a plan to harm the Traders but she had no idea what it was. All she could do to help the Traders was warn them that something bad was going to happen tomorrow.

She sneaked back up the tunnels.

'There you are!' Frida came hurrying towards her, shaking her head in exasperation. 'Vanna sent me to find you – don't you know it's time to eat? Come on, we're waiting for you.'

'But I have to…'

Frida put her hands on her hips, her face stern. 'Vanna said I was to fetch you immediately.' She looked so like the Headwoman that Tia laughed, even though she was worried about the Traders.

'All right.' Frida would drag her to the castle if she had to, rather than disobey the Headwoman! Tia would just have to warn the Traders later. And she was hungry. 'I stopped to buy honey cakes.'

Frida grinned. 'Vanna will be sure to forgive you, then – she likes them even more than you and I.'

Frida was right – Vanna ate more honey cakes than anyone else. 'That's the last of them' she said regretfully, finishing off her third. 'What else did you do in town, Sura, besides buy cakes?'

'I went round the stalls – and I saw a very strange man.' Tia described the man in the cloak. 'I think someone called him Bragi.'

'He leads the bandits!' Frida said. 'They raid travellers, and the Traders' trains too.'

'Stay away from the likes of Bragi and his band,' Gunnar said sternly. 'They're greedy for money.'

Tia nodded vigorously. Gunnar was warning her that Bragi would capture her for the reward if he could. But now she knew that the cloaked man was a bandit chief, she had to warn the Traders as soon as possible. Hyldi and Bragi were both angry with them; they must be plotting to raid them in revenge.

She'd wait until Vanna, Gunnar and Frida were asleep then creep out and tell the Traders what she knew.

When the moon shone brightly through Tia's window she crept into the town. The revellers and night-hawks were too busy enjoying themselves to notice her as she sped to the Traders' camping ground in the shadow of the city walls.

'No!' She stared aghast at the deserted ground. Only moonlit rings and lines of squashed grass showed where the Traders had pitched their tents and tethered their horses. They'd been wise enough to leave early, perhaps in fear of Hyldi's anger over the bronze horse.

Tia wasn't the only one taken aback by the empty spot. Bragi was there with a band of mounted men.

'They travel slowly with their waggons,' he snarled. 'We can catch them up in the Alda valley – they always go that way to Roornhof. We'll ambush them where the valley turns and narrows. It's the perfect place.'

The bandits wheeled away.

Tia could think of only one thing to do. She headed for the stables.

'Yufa?' she called outside the box-stall.

The mare's head jerked up in surprise. 'What's the matter?'

Tia hurriedly explained. 'We have to help the Traders,' she said.

'Of course!' Yufa scraped at the ground. 'We can't let bandits hurt them.'

Tia opened the stall and took down the reins. 'We have to overtake the bandits and reach the Traders before they do. Then we can tell the Traders about the ambush and they can get ready to defend themselves.'

Yufa danced in excitement. 'We can run like a comet through the night!'

Tia calmed the excited horse and led her through the streets. They kept to the shadows so that Yufa's golden hide didn't gleam too brightly in the magical lights of the town. Tia let out a sigh of relief as they passed safely through the gates.

She mounted Yufa. 'The path's stony, we need to go carefully until we pass the volcanoes and reach the valley. Then we can gallop along the grass and overtake the bandits.'

Yufa picked her way carefully and steadily down the moonlit track.

'Wait!' Tia hauled on the reins.

There, sitting in the middle of the path ahead, invisible except to Tia's witch-sight, was Finn. He looked very pleased with himself.

Chapter Eight

The Battle of Alda Valley

'Oh no!' Tia groaned.

Finn's face fell.

'What's the matter?' Yufa asked.

'I've seen something in the road. Wait here.'

Tia slid from Yufa's back, dropped the reins, stooped as though she were examining the ground and made her way to Finn. His camouflage was perfect. From the moon-washed, milky white path to the shadows of bushes and rocks, he matched his background exactly. If Tia hadn't been a witch-child he'd have been invisible to her too.

She crouched in front of him and pretended to prod at the road. 'What are you doing?' she whispered. Even though she was pleased to see her beloved DragonBrother, she was still angry that he'd put himself in danger by passing through the spell boundary for no good reason.

'I'm practising my disguises,' he whispered back. 'I didn't expect to see you.' He nudged Tia with his nose and blew a faint wisp of sweet smoke over her. 'I missed you, DragonSister.'

'I missed you too.' She had her back to the horse, so she was able to stroke Finn's nose without Yufa seeing her do it. 'But you have go back. If you make even one tiny mistake the spell will catch you.'

'I won't…'

'You might,' Tia insisted. 'Go back.'

'All right,' Finn agreed. 'But first tell me what you're doing outside the town at night. That's dangerous too.'

Tia thought that was fair. She told him quickly, prodding the ground all the time as if she were muttering to herself about something she'd found there.

When she'd finished, Finn told her he'd seen a band of men riding towards the western side of the valley. 'You'll need to hurry if you're going to catch up with them,' he whispered.

'I will.' Tia quickly kissed Finn and stood up. 'And now you have to fly away.'

'All right.' Finn took off, his scaly skin changing to match the starry sky as he rose.

Tia went back to Yufa.

'Did you find anything?' the horse asked as Tia grasped a tuft of the white mane and pulled herself onto Yufa's back.

'Yes – the bandits left signs as they went. I know which direction they're going in now.'

Yufa accepted what Tia said and trotted steadily down the road. They soon reached the wooded valley – and the end of the spell boundary. It shimmered across the top of the valley, as delicate as spider silk and just as dangerous.

'The bandits have gone along the west side of the valley,' Tia said. 'The Traders have followed the track down the middle. We'll ride along the eastern side.'

Yufa broke into a canter, then a gallop. She raced along the grassy top of the valley so fast that Tia's cap flew off and went whirling away.

At last Tia spotted the line of bandit horsemen, their dark shapes outlined in moonlight.

'We've caught up with them, now let's pass them,' she urged the little mare. Yufa flew along faster than before and soon left the bandits behind. She caught up with the Traders just as they were nearing a bend in the valley far below.

'That's where Bragi and his band are planning to attack,' Tia said.

'Then let's go and warn them!' Yufa turned down the sloping side of the valley without waiting for Tia to guide her. As soon as she was sure of her footing, she galloped. Tia gripped hard with her knees and lay along Yufa's neck. She was certain the mare was going to stumble as she careered down the valley, dodging bushes and trees, slithering on the damp grass. But Yufa was sure-footed as well as fast and they arrived at the head of the train breathless and unharmed.

Tia reined Yufa in.

'Bragi and his bandits are on their way to attack you,' she told the astonished Traders. She pointed into the narrowing curve of the valley. 'They plan to ambush you there. I heard them plotting. Hyldi's hired them.'

The Traders took in Tia's clothes and the little horse and didn't stop to question her. They quickly began to organise themselves. Most of them disappeared into the shadowy trees; others drew their waggons close together and told the children to stay hidden inside. Two Traders unfastened a wheel from beneath a waggon and propped it up against the side.

'We're pretending we've stopped to replace a broken wheel,' a man told Tia grimly. He drew out a short sword. 'But when they come down on us, we'll be ready for them – thanks to you, whoever you are.'

'I'm Nadya,' Tia said without thinking.

'Ah, the girl the High Witches want so badly,' the man said. 'The bandits will try to catch you and claim the reward. You must go before they get here.'

It was too late for that. Blood-curdling yells split the air, hooves thundered and blades glinted in the moonlight as Bragi and his bandits charged on the Traders.

The men by the waggon wheel spun round, swords at the ready. Others ran out from the trees to attack the bandits from behind. Men and women yelled and swords clanged as the fight went back and forward. First the Traders were winning, and then the bandits.

Tia saw the Trader who'd told her to leave grappling desperately with Bragi. The Trader held off the bandit chief and shouted, 'Go, girl, now!'

Bragi turned in surprise to see who the Trader was calling to. The Trader took advantage of Bragi's loss of concentration and knocked him to the ground.

With a yell of, 'I've got their chief!' the Trader roped Bragi and hauled him to his feet.

The other bandits panicked and tried to run but the Traders overpowered them. They soon had them tied up and bundled into an empty waggon with their chief.

The Trader leader took hold of Yufa's reins. 'It's not safe for you to go back to Askarlend town,' he said to Tia. 'Why don't you travel on with us to Roornhof?'

Tia shook her head. 'I have things to do there.'

'I see.' The Trader let go of the reins. 'Then good fortune go with you.'

'Thank you.' Tia turned away from the Trader train and began to make her way back to Askarlend.

Chapter Nine

Firefight

The volcanoes smouldered ominously in the dawn light as Tia rode towards Askarlend town. Their red glow reminded Tia of the ruby. *I'm no closer to stealing it*, she thought gloomily. She didn't even know where Hyldi kept the comb when she wasn't wearing it.

As Yufa plodded towards the town walls, Tia's gloom deepened. She wasn't any nearer to reuniting the little mare with Shandor either.

A clatter of hooves jolted her out of the dark thoughts. The stable hands were riding the horses out for exercise.

As usual, Kettil was leading the string on the chestnut, Folski. He reined in when he saw Tia. 'Where've you been?' he demanded.

'None of your business.'

Tia tried to ride by but Kettil snapped his fingers and the stable hands surrounded her and Yufa. She scowled at Kettil.

'It's you – that thief on the posters!' Kettil's eyes glittered with excitement and greed.

Tia's hand flew to her hair. She'd forgotten that her cap had fallen off before the fight with the bandits. And the poster showed her scowling. No wonder Kettil had recognised her.

'Ragnar, go and tell the Lady Hyldi I've captured her jewel thief,' Kettil ordered. One of the boys dug his heels into his horse and galloped into the town.

Tia tried desperately to force Yufa out of the circle of horses but they pressed in so closely that Yufa couldn't kick out or back up.

Kettil and the stable hands forced Tia into the town. They stopped in West Gate Square, in front of the troll statue. Loki was perched on its shoulder.

He can't help me now, Tia thought.

People poured excitedly into the square as news of 'Nadya's' capture spread. They jostled and shouted, startling the horses into breaking the circle round Tia. Hands grabbed her, dragged her from Yufa's back. The little mare, eyes rolling wildly, kicked out.

'Get out of the way!' Vanna's loud voice ordered, and her strong arms lifted Tia up. Gunnar grabbed Yufa's reins. She reared.

'It's all right – stay with the man!' Tia called, and Yufa stood trembling, her hide twitching.

Voices shouted, 'Make way for the Lady Hyldi!' The witch's guards forced their way through the crowd to Tia. The High Witch stormed after them.

'So,' she snarled at Tia, 'you are the little thief. I see it clearly now. Where are my sisters' jewels – the emerald, the opal, the topaz and the sapphire?'

'I haven't got them,' Tia said.

Hyldi beckoned and Tia felt herself magically jerked forwards, step by step till she was face to face with the witch.

Hyldi grabbed the front of Tia's shirt and her chain spilled out revealing the emerald, shining a vivid green in the morning sun.

The crowd gasped. Hyldi's eyes widened greedily and she reached for the jewel.

Yufa wrenched herself from Gunnar and cantered straight for the witch. She snaked out her neck, sank her teeth into Hyldi's bun, and pulled. The comb came away in her mouth.

Hyldi screamed. 'My ruby!' She raised one hand to her hair and threw a fireball at Yufa with the other.

Without thinking, Tia conjured up a stream of flames and hurled it at Hyldi's fireball. The two collided and shot into the air in a plume of shrieking fire.

For a second there was a shocked silence then the crowd dived for cover, yelling in terror.

'So, you want a fight, little thief,' Hyldi sneered and threw another fireball.

Tia leapt aside and the fireball hit the troll, knocking its head off. Loki flew away with a squawk of protest.

Hyldi threw fireball after fireball. As Tia dodged them all, Hyldi's aim grew wilder. The battered houses in the square began to smoke, the stalls went up in flames and the troll was reduced to a stump.

At last Hyldi stopped, lungs heaving, to catch her breath.

That gave Tia the perfect chance to hurl a fireball of her own, but she hesitated. She didn't want to fight back with her own fire; it might cause yet more damage to the smouldering houses or hurt someone. But she didn't know what else to do.

Yufa galloped out of a side street where she'd been sheltering and dropped the comb in front of Tia. 'Use this!'

The ruby glowed temptingly at Tia's feet. 'I promised Finn I wouldn't,' she whispered.

'Look out!' the horse warned.

Hyldi was running forward, hair swirling like a nest of snakes, hand stretched out to grab the comb.

Tia snatched it up by the ruby, and felt its crimson power running through her. She pointed the comb at Hyldi. Strands of red light streamed from the jewel and formed a bubble round the witch. It bobbed gently in front of Tia, pulsing red, and Hyldi's frozen expression of furious surprise glared out at her before the bubble drifted off around the square.

Tia sat on one of the troll's gigantic feet and leaned back against the stump of his leg. She was exhausted. Yufa, who had followed her, nuzzled her face comfortingly. Cautiously, people crept out of hiding and into the square. They stared in amazement at the drifting bubble and the witch inside it.

'She hasn't got the ruby any more,' Tia said to them. 'She can't hurt you.'

'No, you've got it,' a man said, looking at the comb Tia was holding.

'And you've got those other jewels as well,' a woman added.

A girl clutched at the woman's arm. 'She could turn into a bear and eat us!'

'Or turn us to ice!'

'Or make us disappear!'

The accusations grew wilder and wilder.

'But I've captured Hyldi for you,' Tia cried, waving her hands in protest. The ruby gave off streams of red light as it moved. The people cried out in fear and scrambled off as quickly as they could. Tia even saw Vanna hurrying Frida away.

Loki fluttered down and perched on the troll's stump. 'They've seen that you're a powerful witch-child and that makes them scared of you,' he said.

It was just what Tia had dreaded. And she was sure Finn would react in the same way when he knew the truth about her.

'At least I can free Shandor,' she told Yufa. 'And the other prisoners.'

'Thank you,' the little horse said. And Tia knew that was the only thanks she would get for defeating the High Witch of Askarlend.

Chapter Ten

To Catch a Thief

In the cavern Tia stabbed the prongs of the comb into the nearest time bubble. It burst in a shower of glittering red dust and a woman dropped to the stony floor. She stared at Tia in bewilderment.

Tia hid the comb behind her back. 'Hyldi's lost the magic ruby and she can't harm you any more.' She pointed to the tunnel entrance. 'That's the way out.' The dazed woman mumbled her thanks and stumbled away.

As soon as she'd gone Tia stabbed the next bubble to glide past. A man fell out of it. Tia gave him the same message, watched him go and then, one by one, released each prisoner. The cavern filled with swirling red dust and Tia's arm began to ache. It took a long time to free all the prisoners. She left Shandor till last.

Tia popped his bubble and he tumbled at her feet. She thrust the comb into her pocket and bent down to help him up. While he shook his head and his mind began to clear, Tia told him about Hyldi, and smiled. 'Yufa's waiting for you.'

Shandor's face lit up with delight and he jumped to his feet. 'Let's go!'

Tia had told Yufa to let Gunnar take her to the stables and sure enough, she was there. Shandor rushed into the stall and flung his arms round the horse's neck.

Tia felt tears prickle her eyes as Yufa whickered happily. She rubbed them away, left the stables quietly and made her way back to her room. She ignored the sideways glances people gave her, and their whispered comments and fearful looks. Hyldi had enjoyed making people feel afraid but Tia didn't.

The minute she reached her room she grabbed her bag from the table, checked that her belongings were still there, slung the bag over her shoulder and left. She didn't try to find Frida, Gunnar or Vanna to say goodbye. She couldn't bear to see distrust on their faces.

Tia, Finn and Loki decided to wait until the next day before setting out on the final quest to recover the pearl from Holmurholt. They lounged idly on a wooded hill overlooking the smoking plains of Askarlend.

Finn bent his long neck round and blinked at Tia as she lay propped against his coppery side. 'You're very quiet. What's worrying you?'

Tia was thinking about the horrified looks the people of Askarlend had given her when they realised she was a witch-child. She couldn't tell Finn she was scared that one day soon he would look at her in the same way.

'Is it because the last witch is your human mother?' Finn guessed.

'No! It doesn't matter to me who Ondine is – I hate all the High Witches,' Tia insisted. 'Freya is my mother, and you are my DragonBrother.'

Finn breathed reassuring smoke over her and she snuggled closer to his cosy, spicy-smelling hide. As she relaxed, a small, niggling doubt entered her mind. She thought she remembered gentle arms holding her, a sweet laugh and a thread of song.

Just for a moment she allowed herself to think, *Perhaps Ondine isn't like her sisters.* After all, the pearl

had the power to heal and mend. Surely Ondine could only use that for good things?

No! Ondine was still a High Witch. She'd find a way somehow to use the pearl to her own wicked advantage.

Many miles away, Ondine looked from her palace window over the lands of Holmurholt. Its rivers glittered in the sun and the stately buildings rising from its dozens of small islands looked as beautiful as ever. Encircling the far-off hills sparkled the spell that defended Holmurholt from dragon attacks. Now there was another threat to Ondine's homeland: a thief who was stealing the jewels of power from the High Witches. At least four had been taken and possibly, by now, a fifth.

As each jewel had been stolen so the spell of protection had grown weaker. It was still powerful but perhaps not powerful enough.

The pearl that hung from a diadem around Ondine's head began to glow as she concentrated. She closed her eyes. Ah yes! The pearl showed her a fragile place in the spell. The gem glowed steadily brighter and the damaged spell began to mend. Soon it was as strong as when it was first made.

Satisfied, Ondine opened her eyes and turned back into her room. The sheen on the pearl dimmed. Now she had mended the dragon spell, she needed to conjure up a completely new one.

Ondine pressed her lips together in a tight, grim line. No little Trader thief was going to take her pearl. It was the dearest thing in the world to her. She picked up one of her books of magic and turned the pages. Ah, there it was: A Spell to Catch a Thief.

Can Tia and her friends meet the challenge of
the final adventure? Find out in

The Pearl Quest

published by Bloomsbury
July 2014